...e Home,
ANNA
HIBISCUS!

by Atinuke

illustrated by Lauren Tobia

WALKER
BOOKS

This is a work of fiction. Names, characters, places and incidents
are either the product of the author's imagination or, if real,
used fictitiously. All statements, activities, stunts, descriptions,
information and material of any other kind contained herein are
included for entertainment purposes only and should not be
relied on for accuracy or replicated, as they may result in injury.

First published 2012 by Walker Books Ltd
87 Vauxhall Walk, London SE11 5HJ

2 4 6 8 10 9 7 5 3 1

Text © 2012 Atinuke
Illustrations © 2012 Lauren Tobia

The right of Atinuke and Lauren Tobia to be identified as
author and illustrator respectively of this work has been asserted by
them in accordance with the Copyright, Designs and Patents Act 1988

This book has been typeset in StempelSchneidler and Lauren

Printed and bound in Great Britain
by Clays Ltd, St Ives plc

British Library Cataloguing in Publication Data:
a catalogue record for this book is available from the British Library

ISBN 978-1-4063-2081-7

www.walker.co.uk

To my husband, Henry
A.

To Jayne,
here's to seed catalogues
and allotment coffee
L.T.

Welcome Home

"Wake up, Anna Hibiscus!" "Welcome home, Anna Hibiscus!" "Wake up!" "Wake up!"

Anna Hibiscus opened her eyes. Jumping up and down on her bed were her cousins Chocolate and Angel.

7

Anna Hibiscus bounced up. She was so
glad to see her cousins, so glad to be back
in the room they shared, so glad to be
back in the big white house, so glad to be
back in Africa, amazing Africa!

Anna Hibiscus shouted, "I'm
back! I'm back! I'm back!"

Double and Trouble came
running into the room.

"Look at my brothers!"
shouted Anna Hibiscus. "They
can run now!"

Anna Hibiscus's mother put her
head into the room and smiled.

"Anna Hibiscus, you fell asleep
on the way home from the airport
and we carried you to bed. Come
downstairs now. Everybody is waiting
to greet you and welcome you home!"

So Anna Hibiscus took off her pyjamas
and put on her pants and her dress.

Getting dressed at home in Africa took no
time at all!

Downstairs, her aunties and
their husbands, her uncles and
their wives and her many-
many cousins were all waiting.

"Welcome, Anna! Welcome
home, Anna Hibiscus!" they
shouted all at once.

Anna Hibiscus had
forgotten her family were so
many! She had forgotten
her family were
so loud!

Then Anna Hibiscus saw Grandfather. He was not shouting. He was sitting quietly on his mat next to Grandmother. He looked small and old. Anna Hibiscus was sure that Grandfather had not been so small or so old when she had seen him one month ago.

Grandfather saw Anna Hibiscus looking at him.

"Welcome home, Anna Hibiscus," he said.

Anna Hibiscus curtsied to Grandfather like a good traditional African girl.

"Greetings, Grandfather," she said.

Grandfather smiled.

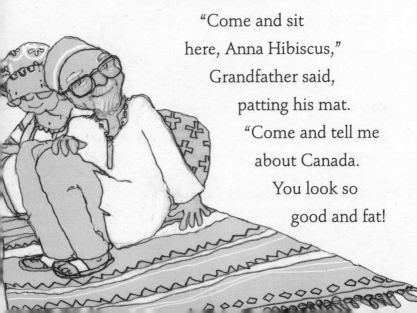

"Come and sit here, Anna Hibiscus," Grandfather said, patting his mat. "Come and tell me about Canada. You look so good and fat!

Did you remember to stay away from dogs, like I told you?"

The whole family laughed. Nobody really believed the rumours about dogs being allowed into houses abroad. Nobody but Grandfather.

Anna Hibiscus opened her mouth but she did not know what to say.

"She has forgotten about Canada already!" Uncle Tunde laughed. "Go and get your camera, Anna Hibiscus. That will remind you."

"Yes! Yes!" shouted Common Sense and Sociable, the big cousins.

"Show us your photographs!" shouted Wonderful and Benz, the boy cousins.

"Then we will see everything!" said Miracle and Sweetheart, the small cousins.

Anna Hibiscus went upstairs slowly. Slowly she came back down with her camera.

"O-ya, come on!" said Uncle Tunde. "Why go-slow?"

Grandfather patted his mat again and all the family gathered around. Uncle Tunde plugged Anna's camera into his laptop and pressed SLIDESHOW.

Uncle Bizi Sunday and Auntie Grace gasped at the pictures of houses covered with snow. Chocolate and Angel licked their lips at the pictures of the cakes that Anna had baked. Double and Trouble clapped at the pictures of Anna sledging down the hill. Anna's mother wiped her eyes and smiled at pictures of Granny Canada and Anna Hibiscus standing with their lanterns in the snow.

Then came a photo of Qimmiq, Granny Canada's dog.

Everybody gasped!

Then came a photo of Anna Hibiscus playing in the snow with Qimmiq! Riding on the snow slide with Qimmiq! Lying on the sofa with Qimmiq!

"WOLF!" shouted Grandfather.

"WORMS!" shouted Uncle Bizi Sunday.

"SMELL!" Clarity held her nose.

Everybody looked at Anna Hibiscus with shocked and worried eyes.

There was a lump in Anna Hibiscus's throat, stopping her from speaking.

"I can explain," Anna's mother said.

But Anna Hibiscus did not wait. Anna Hibiscus ran away.

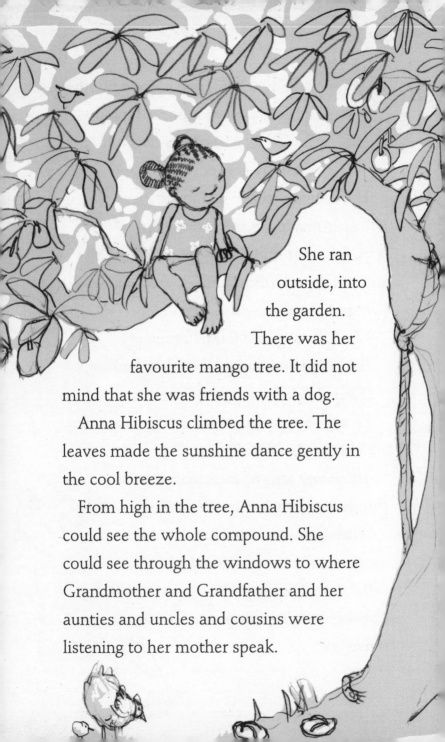

She ran
outside, into
the garden.
There was her
favourite mango tree. It did not
mind that she was friends with a dog.

Anna Hibiscus climbed the tree. The
leaves made the sunshine dance gently in
the cool breeze.

From high in the tree, Anna Hibiscus
could see the whole compound. She
could see through the windows to where
Grandmother and Grandfather and her
aunties and uncles and cousins were
listening to her mother speak.

Anna had been afraid to go to Canada, where everything was new and strange. She had not guessed that coming home would be difficult too.

Anna Hibiscus heard barking. Over the walls of the compound she could see a pack of dogs fighting over scraps in the street.

The dogs were thin and angry. They snarled and barked and bit. Children ran away from them. People shouted. Somebody threw a stone to make them go away.

They are angry because they are hungry, Anna Hibiscus thought. And because nobody takes care of them or loves them.

One month ago I was frightened of all dogs, because I thought that all dogs were like that.

Anna Hibiscus sighed. One month ago
Anna Hibiscus had not understood dogs
and now her family did not understand her.
Did that mean they would stop loving her?
Anna Hibiscus looked down.

On the ground,
beneath the tree,
Anna Hibiscus could
see a chicken. The
chicken was hiding
in the long grass. She
was sitting very still but
her feathers were moving. Then Anna
Hibiscus saw one, two, three, four, five little
chicks' heads peep out from behind
those feathers.

"OH!" shouted
Anna Hibiscus,
and she jumped
straight down
from the tree.

"OH!" she shouted again. Because one month ago she could not jump straight down from the mango tree.

The chicken stood up and walked away. And one, two, three, four, five little chicks followed her.

Grandmother and Grandfather heard Anna Hibiscus shout and saw her jump down from the tree. Grandmother came outside. Grandfather followed.

"Look!" shouted Anna, pointing at the chicken and her chicks.

"My lost chicken!" shouted Grandmother.

"And five more, as well!" Grandfather laughed.

Anna Hibiscus knelt in the grass and looked into the nest. There were the broken eggshells that the baby chicks had hatched from. And there was one whole, unhatched egg!

"Wait!" Anna Hibiscus shouted to the chicken. "You have forgotten one!"

The chicken walked proudly away, leading her babies. She did not look back. Anna Hibiscus's eyes filled with tears.

"Don't worry yourself," said Grandmother. "It is probably a bad one."

"Throw it away!" said Grandfather. "Throw it away!"

Grandmother and Grandfather went back inside, still laughing quietly about the chicken and her chicks.

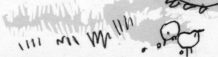

Anna Hibiscus reached into the nest and picked up the egg. It was still warm. She sat down under the mango tree, holding the egg carefully in her hand.

"Anna!" her mother shouted from the bedroom window. "Come and help me unpack your suitcase!"

"Anna!" shouted Uncle Tunde from the car. "I am going with Sociable and Thank-God to print out your photos. Do you want to come?"

"Anna!" shouted Joy from upstairs. "We are doing a project on Canada. Come and help us!"

"Anna!" shouted Auntie Grace. "Come to the sewing room. We want to measure you for a new dress!"

Anna Hibiscus stood up and began to run. She ran first one way and then the other, with the egg still in her hand. Then she stopped running and began to laugh. She was home. And everything was fine. Her family no longer understood her in every way. But they still loved her – one hundred per cent.

Later that night, when projects had been completed and photos printed and dresses cut and suitcases unpacked, Anna Hibiscus and her family gathered on the veranda. Grandmother told a story about how a little girl tamed a wolf by singing sweet songs. Everybody looked at Anna Hibiscus and laughed. And in Anna Hibiscus's hand,

"Cheep! Cheep!"

The cousins gasped, the aunties screamed, the uncles leapt to their feet.

"Anna Hibiscus!" said Grandmother, looking into Anna's hand. "Have you been holding that egg all day?"

"Yes, Grandmother," said Anna Hibiscus.

"I do not believe it," Grandfather said.

And as the whole family watched, the small brown egg in Anna Hibiscus's hand hatched into a tiny white chick.

"Na-wa-oh!" said Chocolate.

"Wow!" said Benz.

"It is white as snow!" said Anna's mother.

Anna Hibiscus looked at the little chick. She smiled.

"Snow White!" she said. "That is your name."

And the whole family laughed. The small white chick was so surprised, it tumbled off Anna Hibiscus's hand. It pecked Auntie Joly's toes. It ran up Uncle Habibi's trouser leg and left a tiny chicken dropping behind. Auntie Joly screamed. Uncle Habibi jumped up. The little chick fluttered onto Uncle Bizi Sunday's arm and tried to pluck out his arm hairs.

Uncle Bizi Sunday shouted and waved his arms. The tiny chick flew onto Anna Hibiscus's head.

"Cheep! Cheep! Cheep! Cheep!" it said.

The whole family looked at Anna Hibiscus with the chick on her head.

Uncle Eldest slowly shook his head. "Trouble dey come," he said.

The aunties nodded. "You speak the truth," they said.

"Bedtime for children," said Anna's mother, smiling.

Anna Hibiscus got up. Auntie Joly tried to take the chick from her head.

"No chickens inside," she said.

"Stop!" said Anna Hibiscus.

The tiny white chick gripped Anna Hibiscus's hair.

23

"Let her take her baby to bed," said Grandfather softly.

"After all, babies belong with their mothers," said Auntie Grace.

"And Anna Hibiscus is the mother," said Chocolate.

"When Snow White grows up and lays eggs, then Anna Hibiscus will be a grandmother!" Sociable laughed.

"How do you know it is a hen?" asked Uncle Tunde. "For all you know, it might be a cockerel!"

"It is too cute to be a boy!" Miracle laughed.

And Anna Hibiscus agreed.

24

Grandfather looked at Anna Hibiscus.
"O-ya," he said. "Take your baby to bed!"
Auntie Joly looked at Grandfather.
"At least it is only a chicken!" he said.

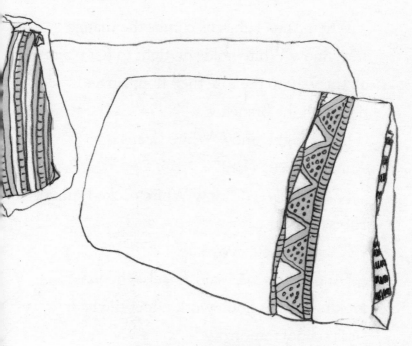

Snow White

Anna Hibiscus is back in Africa. Amazing Africa. Back in the big white house where she lives with her whole entire family and Snow White.

Everywhere Anna Hibiscus goes, Snow White goes too. In the day, Snow White is always on top of Anna Hibiscus's head.

When Anna Hibiscus climbs the mango tree, Snow White holds on tight to her plaits all the way to the top, then hops up and down on the branches.

In the night, Snow White sleeps on Anna Hibiscus's bed.

"Cheep! Cheep!" Snow White pecked Anna Hibiscus's ear.

Anna Hibiscus woke up.

"Anna Hibiscus," said Angel, who was looking for her homework under the bed, "it is school tomorrow."

Anna Hibiscus had forgotten all about school!

"You can't go to school with a chicken on your head!" Common Sense laughed as she shook a towel out of the window.

But Anna Hibiscus could not go to school without Snow White! She never went anywhere without Snow White! Anna Hibiscus ran to her mother.

"Snow White can play with the other little chicks in the garden while you are at school," said Anna's mother.

She looked at Anna's face.

"Don't cry," she said. "I am sure Snow White will enjoy it."

But Anna Hibiscus was not sure.

"Why don't you try after breakfast?" asked her mother.

So after breakfast,
Anna Hibiscus and
Snow White went
into the garden. They
found the chickens scratching
and pecking in the grass. Anna
Hibiscus put Snow White down
on the ground near the other
chicks. Immediately the
mother hen pecked Snow
White. She pecked
and pecked and
pecked. Snow White ran and
hid underneath the bush that Pronto, the old
he-goat, was eating. His foot came down

almost on top of
Snow White!
Anna Hibiscus
screamed. She put
Snow White back
on top of her head

and climbed the mango tree. Anna Hibiscus and Snow White refused to come down for the rest of the day.

The next morning, Anna Hibiscus pushed a crumbled crust of bread and a saucer of water underneath her mother's bed. She untangled Snow White's feet from her hair.

"Cheep! Cheep!" said the little chick crossly.

"You will be safe here," said Anna Hibiscus.

She kissed Snow White and put the chick underneath her mother's bed.

"Beep! Beep!" went the horn on Uncle Tunde's car.

Anybody who was not already in the car would make everybody else late for school! Anna Hibiscus ran downstairs. Everybody could see that Snow White was not on top of Anna's head. So nobody asked any questions.

After school, Anna's mother was waiting
for her on the veranda.

"Your mother looks cross," said Chocolate.

"Very cross!" said Angel.

"Anna Hibiscus!" her mother shouted.
"I need to talk to you!"

"Uh-oh!" said Benz.

Anna Hibiscus walked slowly to the
veranda. Grandmother was sitting
on her mat, making
a basket.

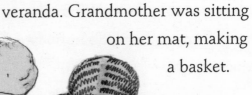

"Follow me!" said Anna's mother.

Scattered all over her mother's bedroom was lipstick and face powder and hair clips. All Anna's mother's special things that normally stood neatly next to the mirror.

"Cheep! Cheep!" said Snow White, fluttering face powder on the bed.

"Sorry, Mama," said Anna Hibiscus in a very sorry voice.

"When you are at school, Snow White goes outside!" her mother said crossly.

Anna Hibiscus looked sad. Snow White rubbed her lipstick-red beak on Anna Hibiscus's cheek.

* * *

33

The next day was market
day. Uncle Bizi Sunday
always went to market.
So Anna Hibiscus shut
Snow White in the kitchen
before she went to school.

Uncle Bizi Sunday was
on the veranda when Anna
came back.

"Uncle Bizi Sunday looks
cross," said Angel.

"Very cross!" said Chocolate.

"Anna Hibiscus!" shouted Uncle Bizi
Sunday.

"U-oh," said Benz.

Anna's feet felt very heavy
when she got down from
the car. Grandmother was
sitting on the veranda.
She was still making
her basket.

"Follow me!" said Uncle Bizi Sunday.

Uncle Bizi Sunday led Anna to the kitchen.

Rice was scattered everywhere. Rice on the table, rice on the floor. Busy pecking in the top of the open rice sack was Snow White.

"Anna Hibiscus, is this your baby?" asked Uncle Bizi Sunday.

"Yes, Uncle," said Anna Hibiscus in a small voice.

"In Africa, when a child is in trouble it is the mother who is to blame," said Uncle Bizi Sunday. "Clear up the rice and don't let me catch this chicken in my kitchen again."

"Sorry, Uncle," said Anna Hibiscus in an even smaller voice.

Anna Hibiscus put Snow White in her
pocket. She swept up all the rice and threw
it outside for the other chickens.
Every time she thought she
had finished, Uncle Bizi
Sunday came in and found
more spilt rice: under
the fridge, behind the
cupboard, in the cracks
in the floor. It took a
long, long time.

Snow White fluttered
up from Anna's pocket
to rub her cheek.

"Oh, Snow White," said Anna Hibiscus.
"What will we do tomorrow?"

The next morning, Anna Hibiscus shut
Snow White in the sewing room. The
aunties would be at work all day and
nobody would go in there.

After school,
Auntie Joly and
Auntie Grace
were standing on
the veranda with
their arms crossed.
Grandmother
was there,
busy with her basket.

"Auntie Grace looks angry," said Angel.

"Auntie Joly looks angrier!" said Chocolate.

Anna Hibiscus said nothing. Her heart was beating fast. She was the last to leave the car.

"Anna Hibiscus!" shouted Auntie Grace.

"Come here now!" shouted Auntie Joly.

Chocolate, Angel, Benz and Wonderful looked at Anna Hibiscus.

"Uh-oh," they said.

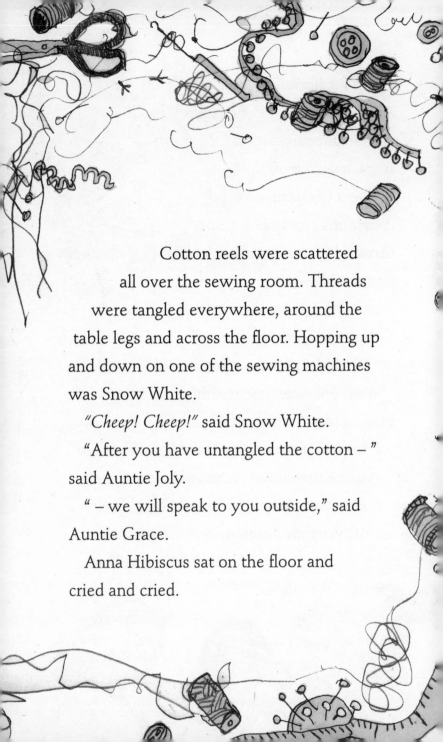

Cotton reels were scattered all over the sewing room. Threads were tangled everywhere, around the table legs and across the floor. Hopping up and down on one of the sewing machines was Snow White.

"Cheep! Cheep!" said Snow White.

"After you have untangled the cotton – " said Auntie Joly.

" – we will speak to you outside," said Auntie Grace.

Anna Hibiscus sat on the floor and cried and cried.

Chocolate, Angel,
Wonderful and Benz put
their heads around the door.
"Uh-oh," they said.

Then Chocolate, Angel,
Wonderful and Benz helped
Anna Hibiscus to untangle the
cotton. It took almost all night.
There was no time for Auntie
Grace and Auntie Joly to talk to
Anna Hibiscus before bed.

"We will talk to you tomorrow!"
they said. "After school."

"My arms are aching," said Chocolate
as they climbed the stairs to bed.

"My eyes are aching," said Angel.

"Maybe tomorrow Snow White can
    play with the other chickens," said
    Wonderful.

    "Snow White is a big chick now,"
    said Benz.

39

Anna Hibiscus said nothing. It was true. Snow White was getting bigger, but not too big to be pecked by hens and trampled by goats.

Anna Hibiscus stroked Snow White's soft feathers as they lay together in bed.

"Don't worry," she whispered. "I will look after you."

The next day Anna Hibiscus did not leave Snow White in the house. But she did not leave Snow White in the compound either. She put Snow White in her lunch box and took Snow White to school.

Anna Hibiscus sang loudly along with the radio all the way so that nobody would hear the *"Cheep! Cheep!"* coming from the lunch box on her lap.

At school, Anna Hibiscus opened her lunch box and put it inside the desk. Then she quickly closed the desk so that Snow White could not jump out.

When the teacher came in, all the children stopped talking and stood up quietly.

"Let us sing our national anthem!" said the teacher.

"Cheep! Cheep!" said Anna Hibiscus's desk.

Chocolate looked at Anna. Benz looked at Anna. The teacher looked at Anna. Anna Hibiscus started to sing loudly and the teacher and all the children joined in.

"Well done, Anna Hibiscus," said the teacher. "You sang well today."

"Cheep!" said Anna Hibiscus's desk.

The teacher looked surprised.

"Thank you!" said Anna Hibiscus loudly.

"You can sit down now," said the teacher. "Let me hear the times tables."

So Anna Hibiscus and all the other children in the class said the times tables. They started well with the two times table. But by the time they arrived at the eight times table, they were struggling.

"You started well," said the teacher. "But you ended poorly. Let me hear the eight times table again."

"Cheep! Cheep!" said Anna's desk loudly.

Chocolate and Benz looked at each other with wide eyes.

"What was that?" asked the teacher.

"Eight times one is eight," said Anna

loudly. "Eight times two is sixteen."

"Good," said the teacher. "Continue, Anna."

"Cheep! Cheep!"

"Eight times three is twenty-four."

Anna Hibiscus stopped. She did not know any more. She had been so busy with Snow White's trouble that she had forgotten to practise.

"I said continue," said the teacher.

"Cheep! Cheep!" said Anna Hibiscus's desk.

"What?" asked the teacher crossly.

Chocolate put up her hand.

"Eight times four is thirty-two. Eight times five is forty. Eight times six is forty-eight. Eight times seven is fifty-six. Eight times eight is sixty-four. Eight times nine is seventy-two. Eight times ten is eighty," she said loudly. Chocolate loved maths.

"Very good," said the teacher.

"Cheep! Cheep!" said Anna Hibiscus's desk.

"Who is making that noise?" asked the teacher crossly.

The whole class looked at Anna Hibiscus.

"DING-A-LING!" rang the school bell. It was time for break.

As soon as the teacher had gone, Chocolate and Benz came to Anna's desk.

"Anna Hibiscus," said Benz, "what is that noise coming from your desk?"

"Did you bring Snow White to school?" asked Chocolate.

Anna Hibiscus crossed her fingers and shook her head.

Chocolate and Benz fetched Angel and Wonderful. They fetched Joy and Clarity and Common Sense. Anna Hibiscus sat on her desk. She crossed her fingers and shook her head and refused to say anything.

She also refused to open her desk.

"Return to your classes!" said the teacher when she came back and saw the cousins gathered around Anna's desk.

"Tap! Tap!" said Anna's desk. Snow White must be pecking at Anna's sandwich.

"Silence!" said the teacher. "Who can tell me about yesterday's history lesson?"

"Tap! Tap!" said the desk again. The teacher looked at Anna Hibiscus. "Put up your hand if you want to speak," she said.

"Tap!" said the desk loudly. The teacher frowned.

Quickly Anna Hibiscus put up her hand.

"OK, Anna Hibiscus," said the teacher. "Come to the front and tell us about yesterday's lesson."

Slowly Anna Hibiscus got up. Everybody was looking at her. She felt hot.

Suddenly the lid of Anna Hibiscus's desk opened and shut. *Bang!* Snow White could open it now that Anna was not leaning on it.

Some children screamed. Others got up to look. The teacher's eyes bulged.

"It is only my lunch box!" said Anna Hibiscus quickly. "Sometimes it opens."

Snow White's head popped out of the round ink hole in the desk. The teacher fainted.

Anna Hibiscus and Snow White were sent to the headmaster's office.

* * *

When Anna Hibiscus got home, her mother
and father and grandmother and grandfather
and aunties and uncles were waiting on the
veranda.

"I have been speaking to your headmaster,
Anna Hibiscus." Grandfather sighed. "This
kind of trouble makes me feel old."

A big lump swelled in Anna Hibiscus's
throat. She had made Grandfather feel old!

Grandmother looked
worried. But she smiled kindly
at Anna Hibiscus.

"Snow White is no longer allowed in the
house," Grandmother said.

Anna Hibiscus's eyes filled with tears.

"It is not traditional," said Auntie Joly.
"And it has caused lots of trouble."

"Our traditions," said Anna's father, "are
there to keep us out of trouble."

48

"What our ancestors learned," said Auntie Grace softy, "we do not have to learn again."

The tears rolled down Anna Hibiscus's cheeks.

"But I understand that you refuse to leave the chick in the compound?" asked Grandmother gently.

Anna Hibiscus nodded.

"The hens peck Snow White and the goats step on her!" She sobbed.

Grandmother held out her basket. She had finished it. It was a big round basket with a lid. Grandmother lifted the lid. There was newspaper in the bottom of the basket.

"This is Snow White's new home," she said. "When you are at school, I will look after her."

Anna Hibiscus's eyes were still crying but her mouth started to smile.

Grandmother smiled even more kindly.

"Cheep! Cheep!" said Snow White and fluttered down to Anna's shoulder to rub against her cheek.

"Snow White is getting big," said Grandmother.

Grandmother held out her hand and took Snow White. Grandmother looked carefully at the big white chick.

"Anna Hibiscus," she said, "your chick is a boy! Snow White is a baby cockerel!"

Anna Hibiscus opened her eyes wide in surprise.

"A boy!" shouted Double.

"Like me!" shouted Trouble.

"No wonder that chicken is so much trouble!" Auntie Joly grumbled.

Everybody laughed.

And Anna Hibiscus stopped crying and laughed too!

Tiger Lily

Anna Hibiscus lives with her mother and her father, her aunties and her uncles, her cousins and her brothers, and her snow-white cockerel. They all live together in the big white house. All except for Snow White. He is supposed to live in his basket or outside.

"My rice!" shouted
Uncle Bizi Sunday in the
kitchen. "Scattered! Again!"

The kitchen door opened and an angry
broom chased out a snow-white cockerel.

"Uh-oh!" said Anna Hibiscus.

She was in the mango tree, reading a book
about how Tortoise cracked his
shell. She saw Snow
White fly straight
into Clarity and Joy,
who were carrying
a basket of wet
washing to hang
on the line. Clarity
and Joy shouted
in surprise.

They dropped the basket
of clean washing.

"Uh-oh!" said Anna
Hibiscus.

54

Snow White ran
around the garden
with a pair of clean
white underpants on his
head. He ran straight underneath
Uncle Tunde's car. Uncle Tunde had his head
under the car. He was fixing something.

"Uh-oh!" said Anna Hibiscus again.

"Ahh-owee!" shouted Uncle Tunde.
He sat up. He had a pair of
dirty white underpants on
his head.

"Somebody catch dis
cockerel!" he shouted.

Anna Hibiscus
jumped down from the
mango tree. She chased Snow White
around the garden.

"Catch'am!" shouted Uncle
Tunde and Uncle Bizi Sunday
and Clarity and Joy.

Snow White flew
into the other chickens.
They squawked loudly and
scattered. The old orange cockerel,
head of the flock, chased Snow White too.

The noise was now so loud that windows
at the back of the big white house opened.
Aunties and uncles and cousins put out their
heads and started to shout.

"Catch'am, Anna! Catch'am!" There was so much squawking and shouting and chasing that nobody noticed the gate opening and a big shiny black car entering the compound. The driver parked the car, and out of the back came a small girl dressed all in pink. Then Snow White came flying around the corner of the house and Anna Hibiscus came chasing him and bumped straight into the small girl.

"Anna Hibiscus!" said the small girl.

"Tiger Lily!" said Anna Hibiscus.

"Ke-ke-re-e-ke-ke!" crowed Snow White,
on the top of the shiny black car.

And around the corner of the house came
Uncle Bizi Sunday and Clarity and Joy and
Uncle Tunde, all chasing and shouting.
But when they saw Tiger Lily, they
stopped in surprise.

There was silence.

The windows at the front of the house
burst open.

"What happen?" shouted Auntie Joly.

"Watin?" shouted Anna's father.

Then they saw Tiger Lily dressed
in pink and the big black
shiny car with the driver
in a uniform sitting in
the front seat.

"Wow!" breathed Benz.

"Introduce your friend," croaked Grandfather, who could see everything from the veranda.

"This is Tiger Lily, my friend from Canada," said Anna Hibiscus.

And everybody stared in surprise because they had not known that people from Canada could have such beautiful brown skin. It was just like Anna Hibiscus's own.

"She is visiting her father here in the city," explained Anna.

"Oh, yes," said Anna's father. "I think we saw him at the airport. Welcome to Africa, Tiger Lily. Is it your first time?"

"Yes," Tiger Lily whispered.

And everybody said, "Welcome! Welcome! Welcome, Tiger Lily. Welcome to Africa!" so many times that Tiger Lily stopped looking shy and smiled. Then Double and Trouble came to hold her hands.

"This is my brother Double," said Anna. "And this is my brother Trouble."

And Tiger Lily laughed.

"Now you must introduce us all," said Grandmother.

So Anna Hibiscus
introduced Grandmother
and Grandfather. And
Tiger Lily curtsied her best
traditional African curtsey
that her father had taught
her, and Grandmother and

Grandfather smiled.

Then Anna
Hibiscus introduced
her aunties and her
uncles.

Tiger Lily curtsied
again and said, "Hello,
Auntie, hello, Uncle," because
she knew it was polite.

And the aunties and
uncles smiled.

Then Anna Hibiscus
introduced her
cousins, big and small.

And Tiger Lily did not curtsey because even the big cousins were not that much older than her.

But she said, "Hello, sister Clarity, hello, brother Sociable." Very politely and Africanly.

Then she said to Anna Hibiscus, "Maybe I should come to play with you another day when you do not have all your family visiting?"

Anna Hibiscus and the cousins looked very surprised but everybody else laughed and laughed.

"They are not visiting," Anna Hibiscus said. "We all live here."

"Everybody?" asked Tiger Lily. "Everybody? All at once? In the same house?"

"Of course!" Anna's father laughed. "Where else would we want to live?"

"And how would we manage on our own?" asked Anna's mother.

"How would we get all the work done without one another?" asked the uncles.

"How would we make decisions without one another's advice?" asked the aunties.

"Who would we play with?" asked the cousins.

"Why else did I build this big house?" asked Grandfather.

"We would be so lonely here alone," said Grandmother. "And how would we keep an eye on everybody?"

Tiger Lily did not know what to say.

"Ke-ke-re-e-ke-ke!" Snow White flew onto the back of Pronto the old he-goat.

"Maaaaaa!" bleated Pronto in indignation.

He leapt into the air and threw his horns back. Then he started to run around the garden.

"Anna Hibiscus!" shouted Grandmother.

"Anna Hibiscus!" shouted her father.

"Anna Hibiscus!" shouted her aunties and uncles and cousins.

"Oh-oh!" said Anna Hibiscus. She grabbed Tiger Lily's hand and started to chase Pronto and Snow White.

Pronto knocked over buckets and kicked over rakes.

"Why are they all shouting at you?" asked Tiger Lily.

"Because I am his mother," panted Anna Hibiscus. "That cockerel is my baby."

Tiger Lily looked at Anna Hibiscus.

"You do not look like a chicken," she said. "I cannot believe you laid an egg."

Anna Hibiscus laughed. She laughed so much that she had to stop running.

Pronto ran straight into the clean washing hanging on the line. His horns caught in a shirt belonging to Grandfather. The shirt tore off the line and flapped from Pronto's horns as he continued to run.

"ANNA HIBISCUS!" screamed Clarity and Joy.

"You must control your chicken!" shouted Uncle Eldest.

"This cannot happen every day!" yelled Auntie Joly.

Uncle Bizi Sunday stood up. "We must do something about this!" he shouted.

Everybody looked crossly at Anna Hibiscus.

Quickly, Tiger Lily took Anna's hand.

"Maybe Anna Hibiscus could play at my house today?" she said.

Anna's mother thought for a moment and then smiled. "Yes," she said.

Then Uncle Bizi Sunday caught Snow White and put him back in his basket. And Anna Hibiscus got into the big shiny black car and waved goodbye.

Anna Hibiscus and Tiger Lily sat
in the back of the big car for a long
time. Now the buildings were tall
and reached the sky. Some were even
hidden in the clouds.

In one of these buildings lived Tiger
Lily's father.

"Na-wah-oh!" said Anna Hibiscus.

Inside the flat where Tiger Lily's father lived, the floors had a thick, soft carpet. Anna Hibiscus could no longer see her feet. She looked for cousins but there were none. She looked for aunties but there were none. She looked for uncles and for grandparents. But there were none.

Then Anna Hibiscus noticed that in every room there was a screen. Instead of people.

"Do you want to watch television?" Tiger Lily asked.

Anna Hibiscus and Tiger Lily lay on the carpet and watched television. There were many different channels.

"Boring," said Tiger Lily. "Boring, boring, boring."

But Anna Hibiscus liked the cartoons, so they watched cartoons for a long time. Then Tiger Lily said, "Boring," and she switched off the screen.

A shy lady brought them some food. She did not speak English or any of the African languages that Anna Hibiscus knew.

Tiger Lily looked out of the window. Anna Hibiscus looked too. Down below, the people looked as tiny as ants. The buses and cars no bigger than cockroaches. The city was as busy as an ants' nest, with as many vehicles as cockroaches in a dirty kitchen.

"Boring." Tiger Lily sighed at last. "Do you want to swim?"

"Oh yes!" said Anna Hibiscus.

So Tiger Lily lent Anna Hibiscus a swimming-costume and a towel, and they went up on the roof to the pool.

The pool was surrounded by chairs and umbrellas of every colour. All around the pool, people were drinking from tall glasses and reading newspapers. Nobody looked happy, even though they were next to a big blue swimming-pool under the big blue African sky.

Maybe it is because they too live alone in empty flats like Tiger Lily's father, thought Anna Hibiscus. They have soft carpets and big screens and no people. Maybe they have forgotten how to smile.

Tiger Lily and Anna Hibiscus were the only children in the pool. They splashed and shrieked and laughed loudly. The other people looked at them and frowned.

"Shh!" they said at last. "You are disturbing us."

Tiger Lily sighed. "Let us go to the shops."

But Anna Hibiscus had no money. Tiger Lily gave half her money to Anna.

"My father will give me more," she said.

73

In the car Anna Hibiscus and Tiger Lily talked about what they wanted to buy. Tiger Lily wanted a new iPod. Anna Hibiscus thought she would be very happy with a doll.

It was a long way in the car.

"Traffic is bad," said the driver.

Anna Hibiscus looked out of the window. The road was jammed with other big shiny cars and busloads of people and taxi-motorbikes with their passengers. Their car was not even moving anymore.

The road was completely blocked.

Suddenly a face appeared at the window. It was the face of a small boy. He was dirty. He looked sick.

"Small money, small money," he begged.

Anna Hibiscus looked at the poor boy. He looked hungry and desperate. She looked at Tiger Lily.

"My father says not to give money," Tiger Lily said. "He says people should work, not beg. He says giving money makes the problem worse."

Anna Hibiscus looked at the boy again. He looked too small and too sick to work.

A face appeared at Tiger Lily's window. A small thin dirty girl. She was begging too.

"Tiger Lily," said Anna Hibiscus, "they look sick. They look hungry."

"Do not worry," said the driver. "We will soon drive on."

Quickly Anna Hibiscus found the window button. She put money into the open hands of the boy. He looked at the money. Immediately he smiled.

"Bless you!" he shouted.

Ten more desperate faces appeared at the open window. Hands were pushing inside the car.

"Oh, Anna Hibiscus!" said Tiger Lily. She sounded frightened.

Anna Hibiscus was not frightened. She put money into each hand. The faces smiled and voices blessed Anna Hibiscus. More and more faces appeared until Anna Hibiscus had no money left.

Anna Hibiscus opened her empty hands. The sad faces turned away. They ran around to the other side of the car. To Tiger Lily's window.

A thin woman with a crying baby was banging on the window. Tiger Lily was crying too. The driver was shouting at the beggars to go away.

Tiger Lily looked at Anna. "I don't know what to do!" she cried.

Anna Hibiscus knew what to do. She opened Tiger Lily's window. Then she took Tiger Lily's money and gave it to the sick mother. The woman could not believe her eyes.

"Bless you," she whispered.

Anna Hibiscus and Tiger Lily shut the windows. They had no money left.

They did not talk. They were thinking of all the faces, all the mothers and children and babies. The people they had helped and those they had not been able to help.

Then Tiger Lily said, "Can we play at your house?"

"Yes," said Anna Hibiscus. "We can help to fix the washing line."

So Tiger Lily and Anna Hibiscus played at Anna's house. With all of the cousins it was so much fun!

"Tiger Lily is so lucky!" said Clarity, after Tiger Lily went home. "To have carpets and Sky television."

"And swimming-pools and air conditioning!" said Benz.

"Her father must be so rich!" said Common Sense.

"I wish we were rich!" Chocolate sighed.

"It is not fair," said Sociable.

Anna Hibiscus said nothing.

Grandmother looked at Anna Hibiscus.

"How about you, Anna Hibiscus?" she asked. "Don't you wish we were rich?"

"I don't know," Anna Hibiscus said. "The rich people I saw did not look happy. They looked so serious. As if they had forgotten how to laugh."

Grandfather chuckled his old man's chuckle.

"It is a serious thing to be rich," he said.

"You can buy swimming-pools and carpets and television screens," said Grandmother, "but you cannot buy happiness."

"But I do not want to be poor," said Anna Hibiscus. "I do not want to be sick and hungry and frightened."

Grandmother and Grandfather were silent.

"I am happy to be myself," said Anna Hibiscus. And she went to find Snow White. He was probably in trouble.

Anna's Stories

Anna Hibiscus is so glad to be back with her whole entire family in the big white house. Grandmother and Grandfather are in charge of everybody in the house. But Grandfather is getting old.

Whenever there is a problem, Grandfather sighs and says, "I am too old for this."

Whenever he says that, Grandmother looks worried and frightened. Anna Hibiscus had never seen Grandmother look frightened before. She had never seen Grandfather look old before. Before she went to Canada, Grandfather never looked old and Grandmother never looked frightened. They became old and frightened when she was away.

Anna Hibiscus was squatting in the dirt with Tiger Lily. Tiger Lily was drawing pictures with a stick. But Anna Hibiscus was looking at the veranda, at Grandmother and Grandfather.

"Anna Hibiscus!" shouted Auntie Joly. "Come and help your aunties!"

"O-ya, Tiger Lily, you can come too!" shouted Auntie Grace.

Tiger Lily came to play every day and she did not mind working hard too. When Anna and her cousins hid from the aunties it was Tiger Lily who said, "O-ya, come on! It's fun to help!"

The aunties were washing clothes in big tubs near the outside tap. Anna Hibiscus and Tiger Lily splashed and scrubbed until they were wet too.

"My mother has a washing machine," Tiger Lily said. "That is not as much fun as this."

The aunties laughed.

"When we are in the village we wash our clothes in the river," said Auntie Grace.

"Cool!" said Tiger Lily.

"Cool!" said Anna Hibiscus.

"Cool, if you don't mind crocodiles," said Auntie Joly.

"Anna Hibiscus!" shouted Sociable.

"Tiger Lily!" shouted Thank God.

Tiger Lily and Anna Hibiscus ran to help the big boy cousins catch baby goats. The goats were high in a guava tree, eating the precious guavas.

"This is so fun!" panted Tiger Lily, catching a small goat by the tail.

"If you want this kind of fun you should go to the village." Sociable laughed.

"There you can chase goats all day."

"Cool!" said Tiger Lily.

"Cool!" said Anna Hibiscus, hanging from a branch.

"Cool, if you don't mind dodging snakes!" Thank God laughed.

"Anna!" shouted Anna's father.

"Tiger Lily!" shouted Uncle Tunde.

"Come and help us!" shouted Uncle Eldest.

Anna Hibiscus and Tiger Lily gave the baby goats to Sociable and Thank God to put back in their pen. They ran across the compound to where Anna's father and the uncles were looking at a broken radio.

"See this broken wire?" Uncle Eldest pointed.

"Screwdriver," said Anna's father.

Anna passed him the screwdriver.

"Wire cutters," said Uncle Tunde.

Anna pointed at the wire cutters and Tiger Lily passed them.

"Soldering iron!" shouted Uncle Habibi.

Together Anna Hibiscus and Tiger Lily passed the soldering iron.

"This is fun." Tiger Lily laughed. "Before I came here I did not know how to fix things."

"You should go to the village," said Anna's father, "if you like fixing."

"Yes," agreed Uncle Eldest. "In the village everything is old."

"So we are always fixing, fixing, fixing..." concluded Uncle Tunde.

"Anna! Tiger Lily! Come and play!"
shouted Benz.

"Now! Now! Now!" shouted Double
and Trouble.

Anna Hibiscus
and Tiger Lily ran and played with Angel
and Chocolate and Benz and Wonderful and
Miracle and Sweetheart and Double and
Trouble and even Clarity and Joy and
Common Sense. They were playing with
bottle tops. They took it in turns to throw

their tops at a pile and win some more.

"This is so-so fun!" Tiger Lily laughed.

"If you think this is fun," said Joy, "you should go to the village."

"They know so many games there!" said Clarity.

"Anna! Anna Hibiscus!" Grandmother was calling.

Grandfather and Grandmother had lost their magnifying glass. They could not read the newspaper without it. Anna Hibiscus and Tiger Lily looked and looked but they could not find it.

"In the village," Grandfather sighed, "there is no newspaper with small-small words."

"Or pages large and unmanageable as bed-sheets," said Grandmother crossly.

"What do you do in the village," asked Tiger Lily, "instead of reading newspapers?"

"We tell stories!" Grandmother chuckled. "Good ones!"

"And we talk to the other elders," said Grandfather.

"Where is the village?" Tiger Lily asked politely.

"*Our* village," said Grandmother, "is far from here. It is near the capital of our people's kingdom."

Anna Hibiscus had heard this before. That was the village where Grandmother and Grandfather had both been born. It was where they had married and where the uncles and aunties had been born before Grandfather's work had brought them all to the city. It was the place where all Anna Hibiscus's ancestors were buried.

"Where is your village, Tiger Lily?" asked Grandmother.

"I don't have a village," said Tiger Lily.

Grandmother and Grandfather frowned.

"Tiger Lily is from Canada," said Anna Hibiscus. "They do not come from villages there."

"We all have a village," said Grandfather. "It is where everybody lived before there were cities."

"I was born in the city," said Tiger Lily. "I don't think there are any villages left in Canada."

Grandfather sighed and looked old. Grandmother looked worried. Anna's mother came running out onto the veranda, holding her mobile phone.

"Tiger Lily's father is coming to greet us," she said. "Now-now!"

The aunties all ran to change into their finest bubas and wrappas. They tied on their biggest, stiffest head ties.

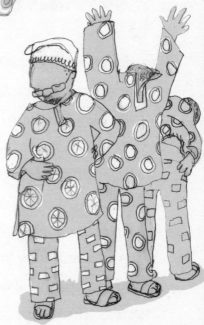

The uncles also changed into long clean shirts and cool trousers. Anna Hibiscus, Tiger Lily and the cousins washed their hands and faces and feet.

Everybody gathered on the veranda.
There were cold soft drinks with ice and
fried plantain dodo, like chips but sweeter.
Everybody knew that Tiger Lily's father was
a big, important man. They wanted to greet
him in style.

"Just like a party!" said Tiger Lily.

And everybody laughed.

"A real party," said Grandmother, "takes
at least three days to prepare."

"In the village," said Uncle Habibi, "it
takes over a week!"

"I want to go to the village!" said Anna.

"Me too!" said all the small cousins.

And the aunties and uncles laughed.

"Why have you not been there?" asked Tiger Lily. "I thought it was your village."

"It is too far," said the uncles.

"And too hot," said the aunties.

Then the gates opened. A limousine with a flag flying on the front drove into the compound. Behind it came another, more ordinary car. Men jumped out of the ordinary car. One of them opened the back door of the limousine and Tiger Lily's father stepped out.

The aunties
and the uncles
stepped
forward to
greet him. They
had smiles on
their faces.
Their clothes
shone stiffly and smartly in the sunlight.

Then out from behind the hibiscus bushes
flew a flash of white.

"Ke-ke-re-e-ke-ke!"

With his talons outstretched, Snow White
flew straight down onto the head of Auntie
Joly. Auntie Joly was wearing the biggest,
stiffest head tie of all.

When Auntie Joly felt something land on
her head, she screamed and threw her arms
up in the air.

Snow White flew away again. But he had
Auntie Joly's head tie in his talons!

The aunties and uncles forgot all about greeting Tiger Lily's father. They looked at Auntie Joly with their eyes opened wide. Auntie Joly's hair was sticking out in every direction.

When Auntie Joly saw their faces and her own hands touched her sticking-out hair, she screamed again. Auntie Joly ran back into the house.

Tiger Lily's father and his men were watching with their mouths wide open. As Snow White flapped over them he dropped the head tie onto the heads of the watching men.

They started to run and shout and wave their arms. Some of them bumped into each other and fell down, still shouting.

The uncles covered their eyes. The aunties grabbed one another's arms. Grandmother silently started to pray.

Snow White landed on
the washing line.

"Ke-ke-re-e-ke-ke!"

Tiger Lily's father
looked at
Auntie Joly
running into the
house screaming.
He looked at the
faces of the aunties
and uncles. He
watched his own
men shout and run
and fall down. His own
mouth was wide open.

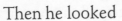

Then he looked
at Anna Hibiscus and
Tiger Lily. Their eyes
were opened wide and
their hands covered
their mouths.

Slowly Tiger Lily's father started to laugh. He laughed and laughed and laughed. He laughed so hard that the aunties and the uncles started to laugh too. He laughed so long that Grandmother and Grandfather had to join in.

Tiger Lily's father wiped his eyes.

"Whose is that cockerel?" he asked.

"It is mine, sir," said Anna Hibiscus, forgetting to curtsey.

"Papa, that is Snow White," said Tiger Lily. "Remember I told you about him?"

Tiger Lily's father was still wiping his eyes. He watched his men get up sheepishly from the ground.

"That cockerel could lead a revolution," he said, starting to laugh again.

Then the uncles greeted him and the aunties greeted him and he greeted Grandmother and Grandfather. And the cousins brought him drinks and food. And he thanked everybody for looking after Tiger Lily so well when he was in his office.

When he reminded them all that Tiger
Lily was returning to Canada the next day,
Tiger Lily and Anna Hibiscus cried and cried
and cried and nothing could stop them.
When the limousine – with Tiger Lily inside
it – disappeared from the compound, Anna
Hibiscus cried louder and louder.

"She will come back," said Anna's father.

"And you can Skype her on my laptop,"
said Uncle Tunde.

Anna Hibiscus continued to cry.

"Grandfather looks sad too," said Anna's
mother.

Anna Hibiscus looked at the veranda.
There was Grandfather, sitting alone.
He looked so small and so old and so sad.

"Oh, Grandfather!" Anna Hibiscus's
heart cried. And her legs ran straight to the
veranda.

"Anna!" Grandfather smiled.

Anna Hibiscus sat next to Grandfather.
She leaned her head on his knee.
Grandfather touched the tears on her face.

"It is sad to say goodbye to true friends."
He sighed. "I know."

Grandfather sounded
so sad. Anna Hibiscus
wanted to cheer
him up.

"Shall I help you read, Grandfather?" Anna Hibiscus asked, pointing at the newspaper.

"No, no." Grandfather sighed again. "It is all bad news and I am too old to do anything about any of it."

Then Anna Hibiscus thought of the stories Auntie Jumoke had told her on the plane. Those stories had cheered her up when she was feeling sad. Maybe they would cheer Grandfather up too.

She remembered the story about the boy and the crocodile that was not a crocodile. Anna Hibiscus laughed.

"Now you are laughing, Anna Hibiscus?" said Grandfather, surprised.

Anna Hibiscus told Grandfather the crocodile story.

"That was me!" Grandfather laughed. "When I was a boy and I thought the log in the river was a crocodile. How did you know that story, Anna Hibiscus?"

"Auntie Jumoke told me," Anna Hibiscus said, "on the plane. She told me lots of stories."

And Anna Hibiscus told Grandfather the story about her father getting stuck on a roof when he was a boy, and the one about Auntie Joly losing all her clothes in the river, and about Grandmother being chased by a wild pig through the bush. And Grandfather laughed and laughed and laughed.

"Incredible," said Grandfather, shaking his head. "You went all the way to Canada to learn about village life."

Anna Hibiscus was so happy to see
Grandfather laughing that she told him all
the stories she knew. Grandfather laughed
and Anna Hibiscus cheered up too.

"It is good to hear those old stories,"
said Grandfather when Anna Hibiscus had
finished. "It makes me feel young again."

Anna Hibiscus looked at Grandfather.
He did look younger now.

"I have been feeling old, Anna Hibiscus,"
Grandfather said, sighing. "But
hearing those village stories…"

Grandfather looked at Anna
Hibiscus. Then suddenly he
leapt to his feet like a young
man and banged his cane.

The whole family
came running out
onto the veranda.

"*Ore mi*," said
Grandmother. "What is it?"

"I feel young again!" said Grandfather.
"And I know what to do to stay feeling young!"

"What is it? What is it?" everybody shouted.

"I am going to the village!" announced Grandfather. "For a visit!"

Everybody gasped.

"It is too far!" shouted Uncle Eldest.

"And too hot!" shouted Auntie Joly.

"I am going," said Grandfather. "And that is that."

Anna Hibiscus tugged Grandfather's hand. He looked down at her and smiled. "Anybody who wants to accompany me is welcome," he said.

And Anna Hibiscus smiled too. Grandfather was still old and Anna Hibiscus was still missing Tiger Lily. But their smiles were like rainbows, big and bright and beautiful. Just like Africa.

Atinuke was born in Nigeria and spent her childhood in both Africa and the UK. She works as a storyteller in schools and in theatres, telling traditional African tales. Atinuke is the author of two children's book series, one about Anna Hibiscus and one about the No. 1 car spotter. Atinuke lives on a mountain by the sea with her husband and two young sons.

Lauren Tobia lives in Southville, Bristol. She shares her tiny house with her husband and their two yappy Jack Russell terriers. When Lauren is not drawing, she can be found drinking tea on her allotment. *Welcome Home, Anna Hibiscus!* is her sixth book.